INVISIBLE

Katja Kamm

North-South Books
NEW YORK / LONDON

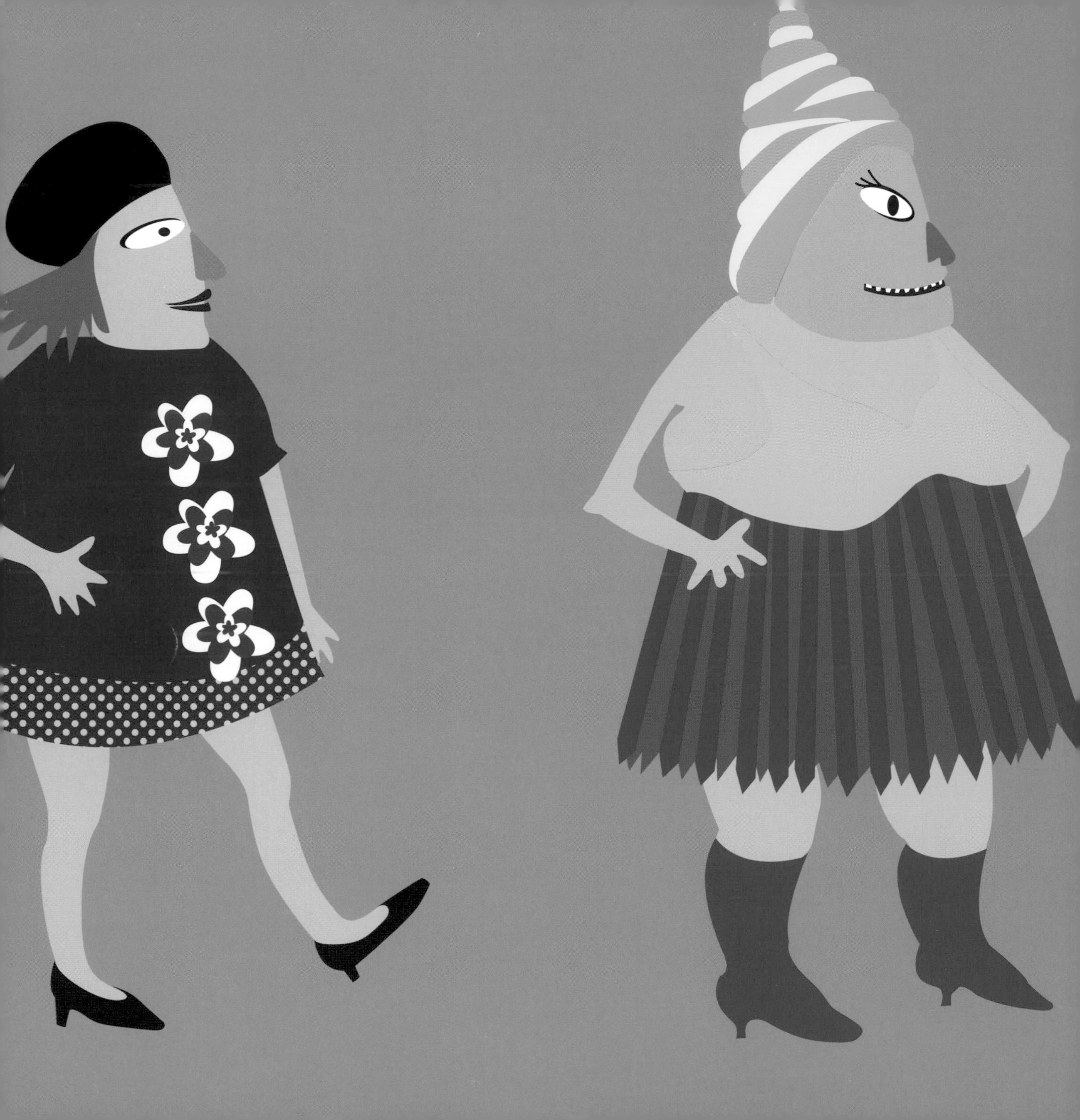

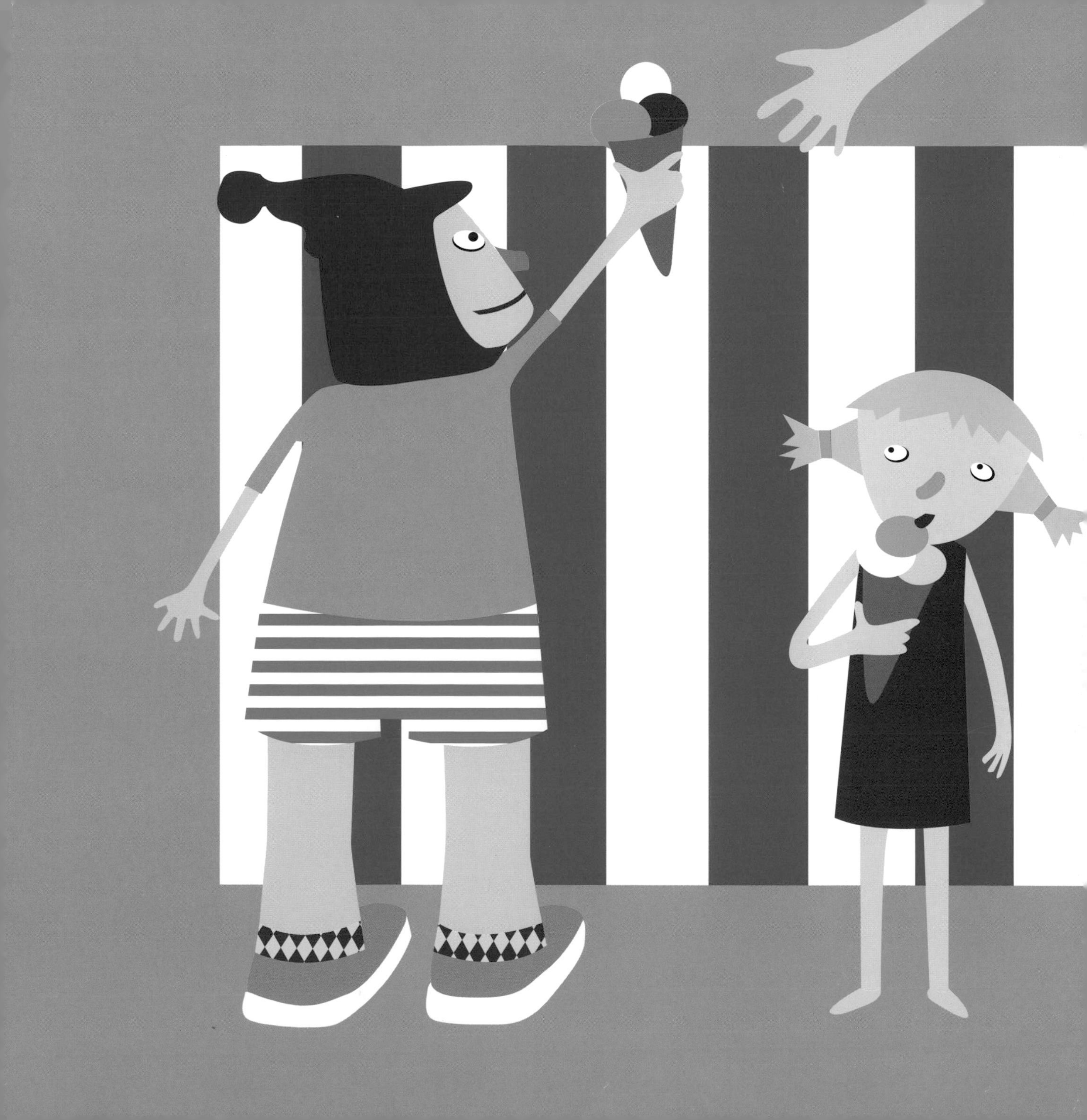

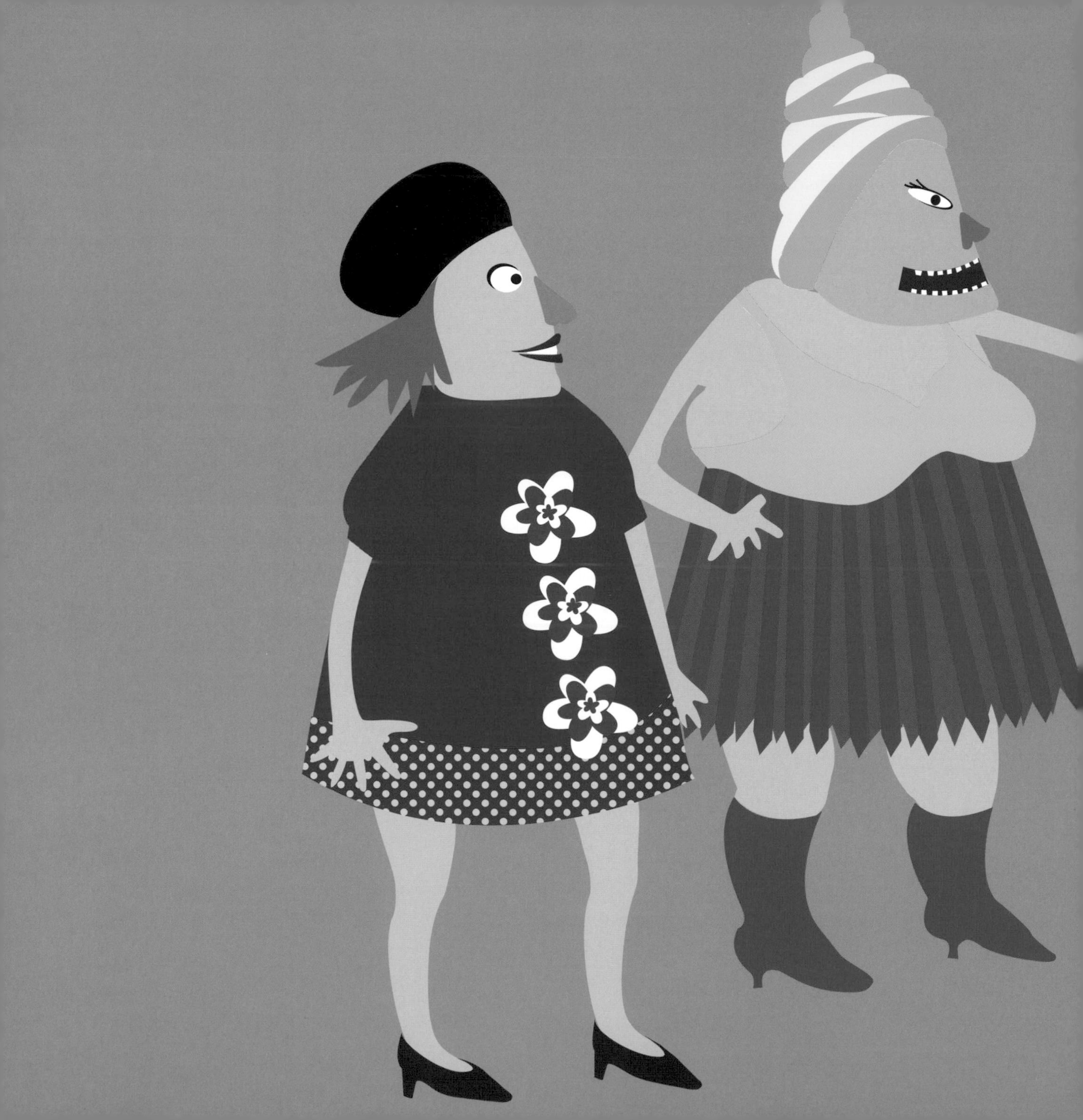

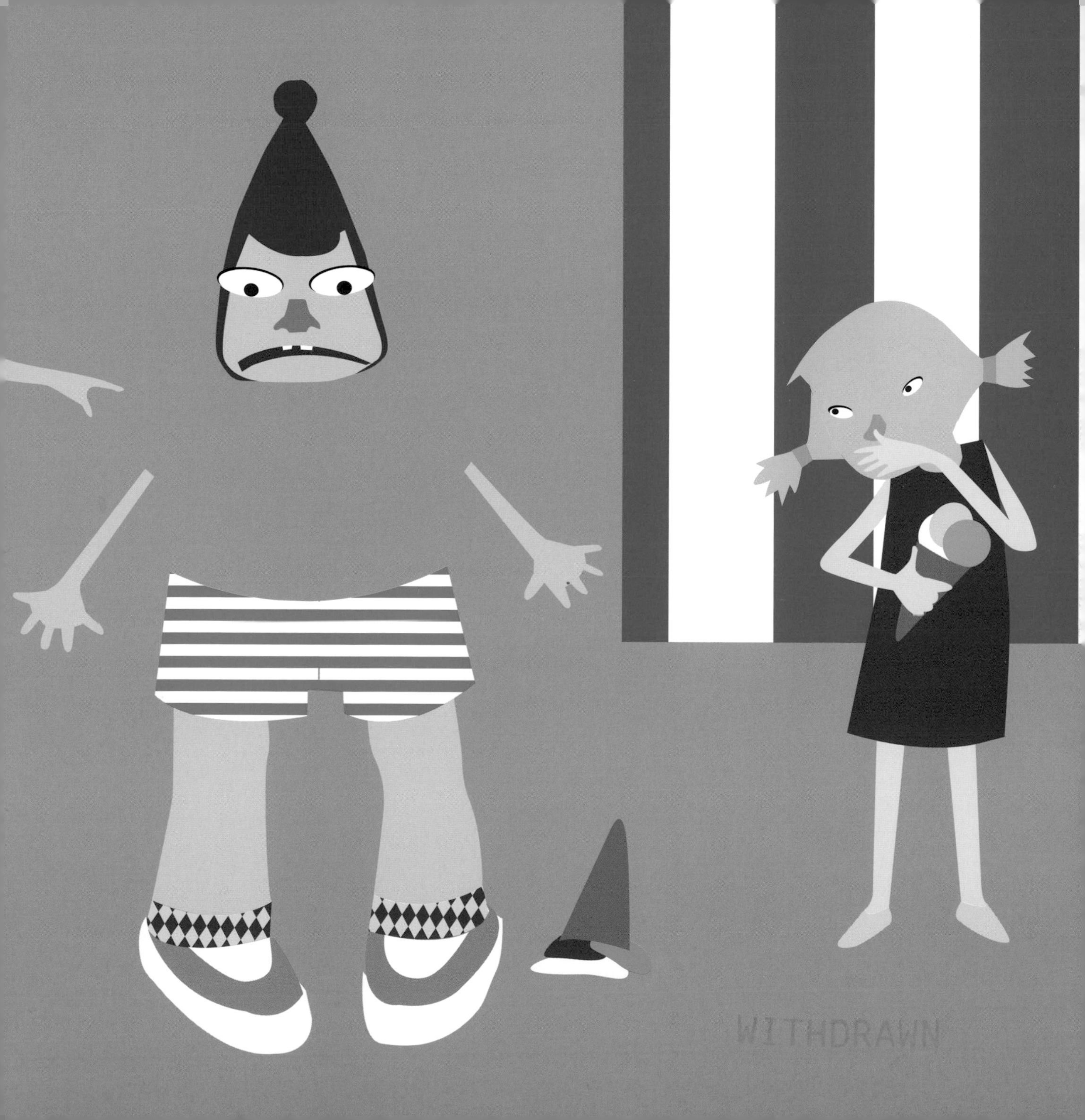

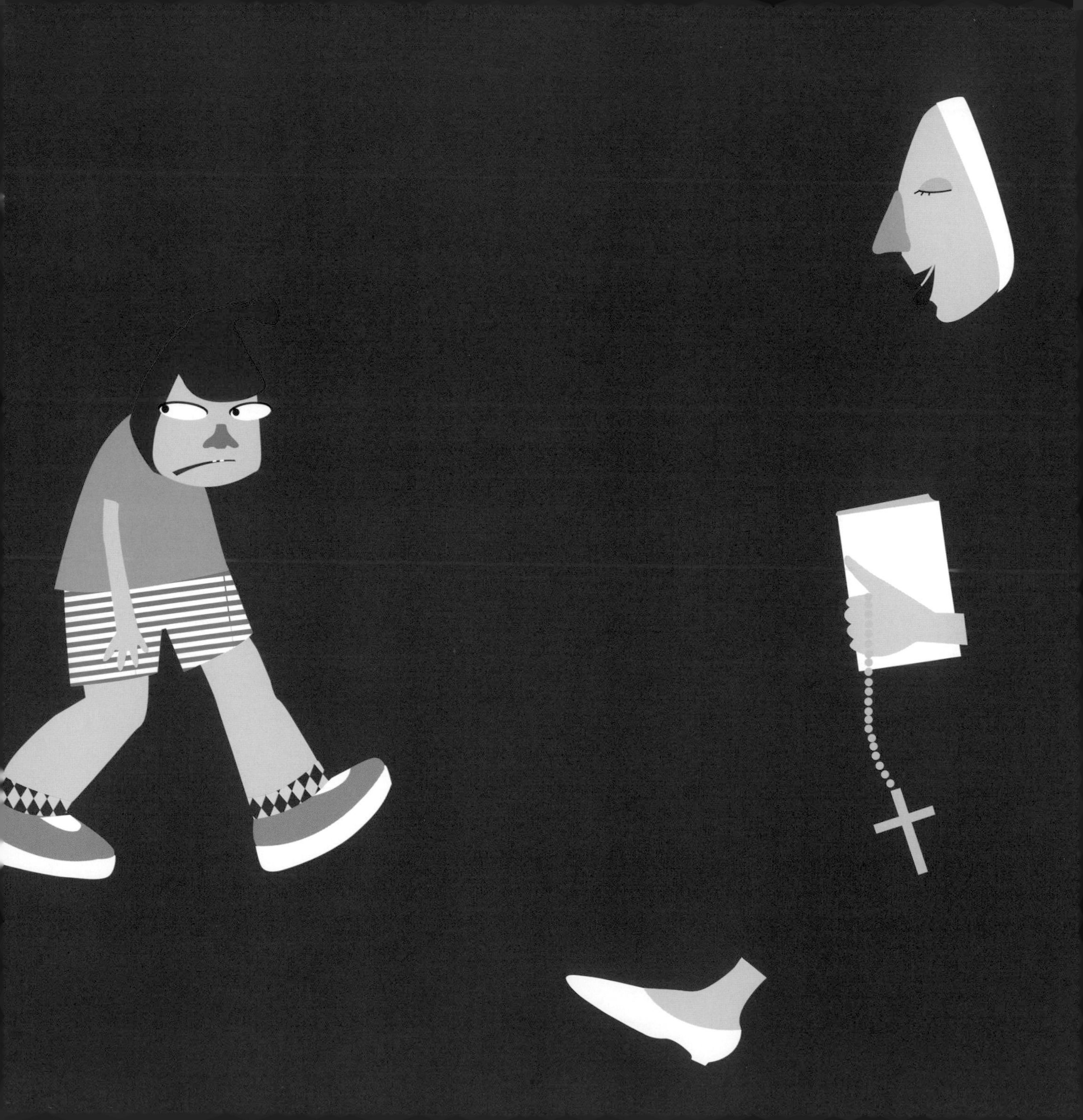

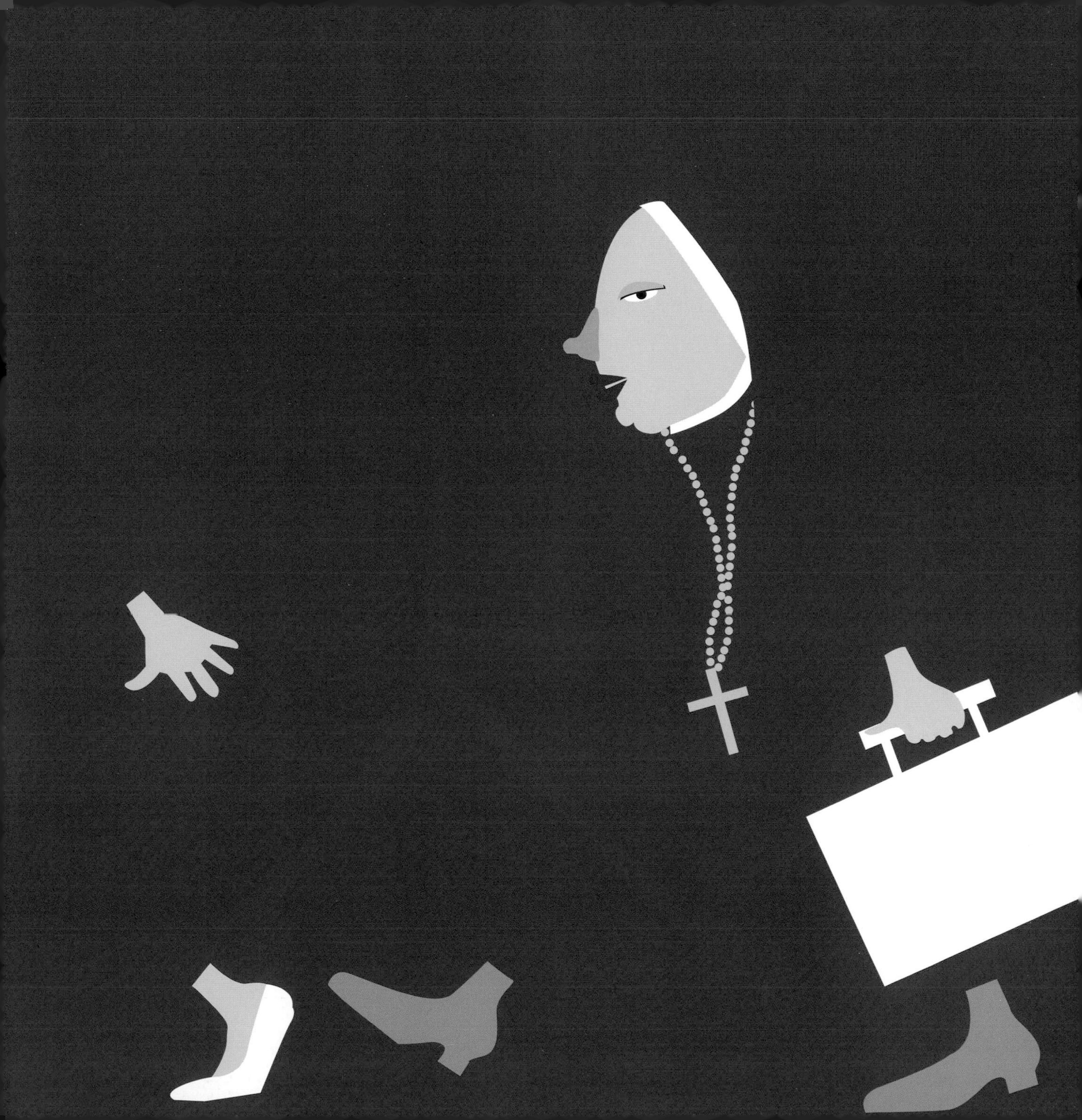

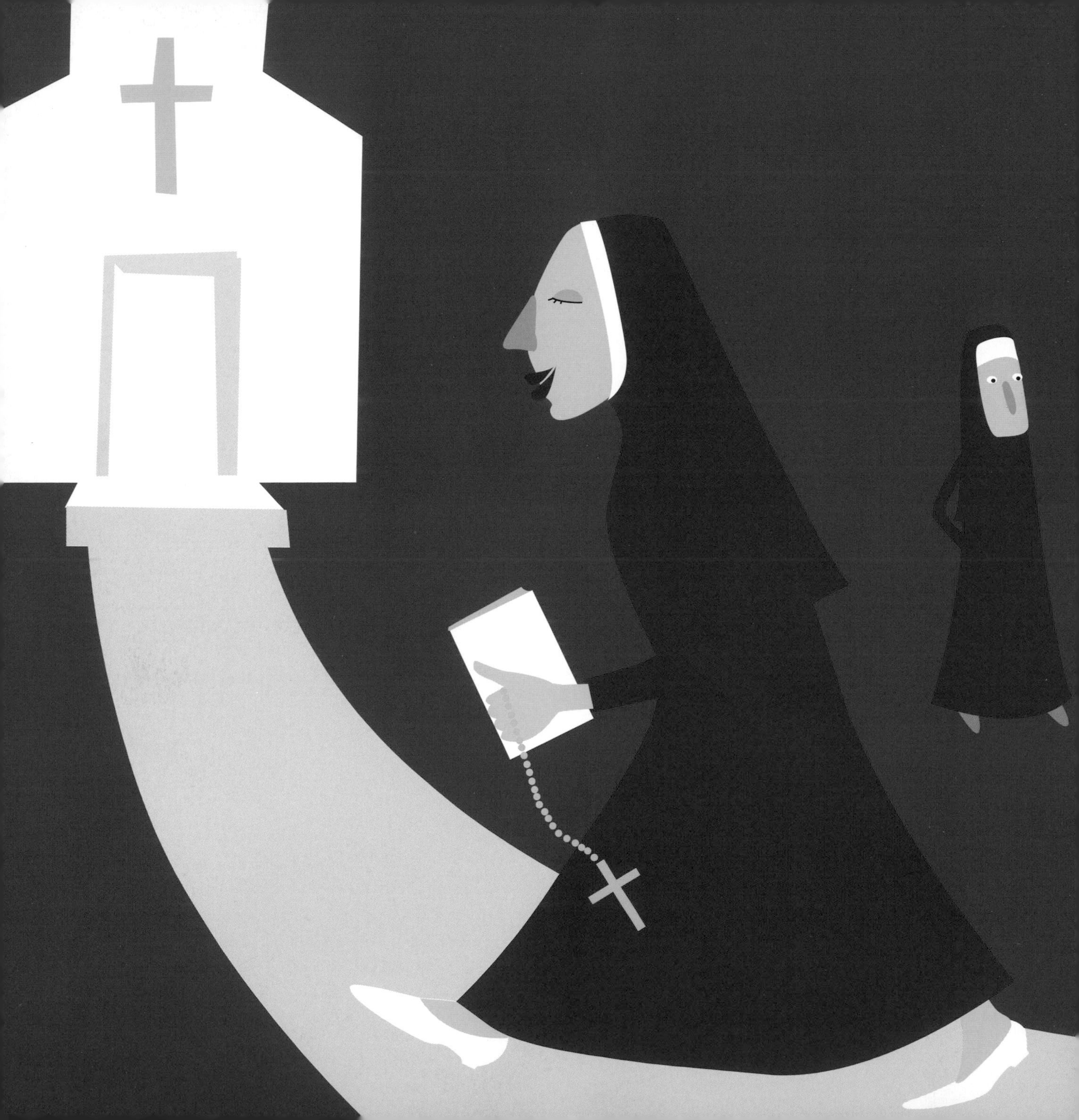

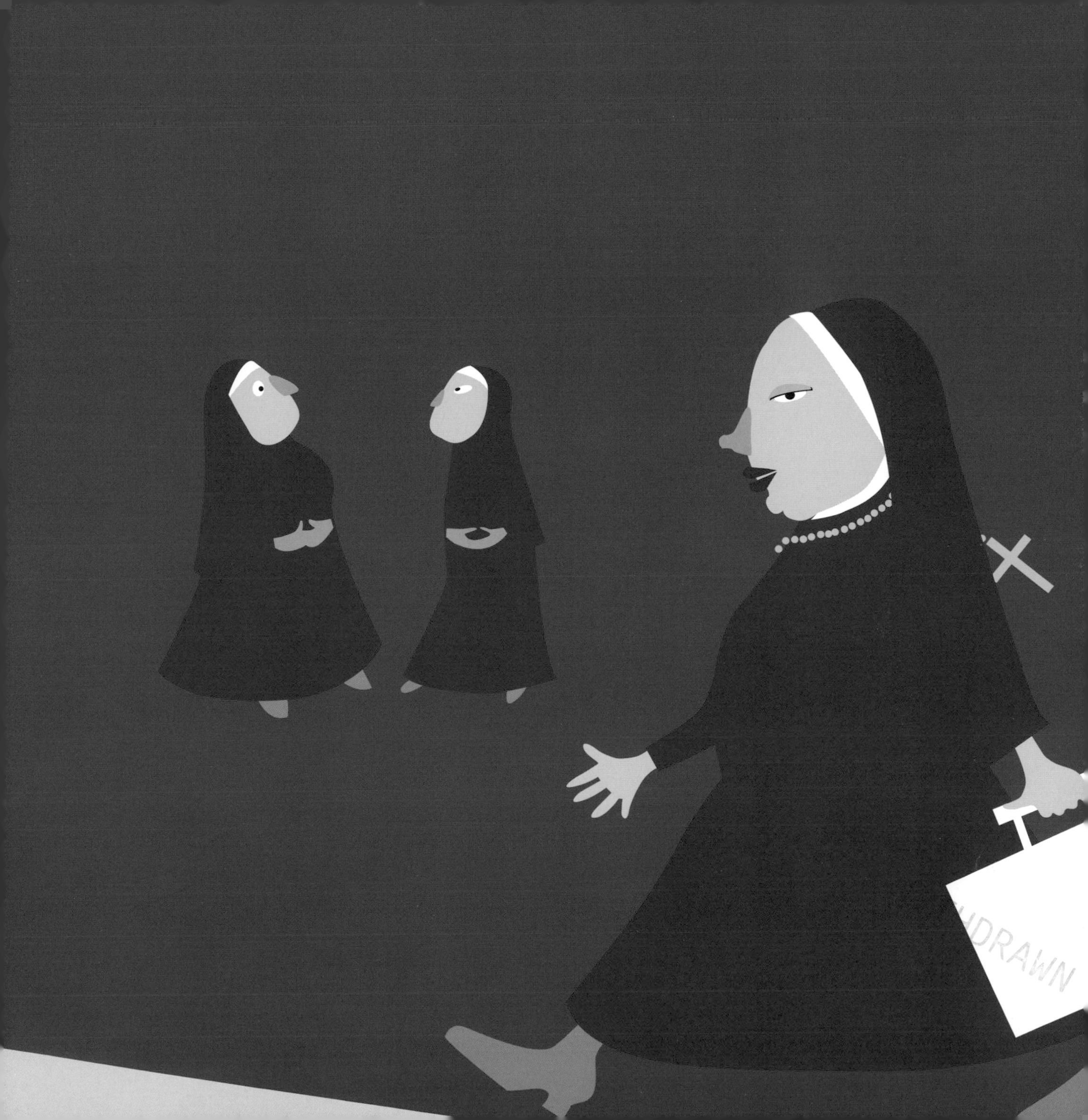

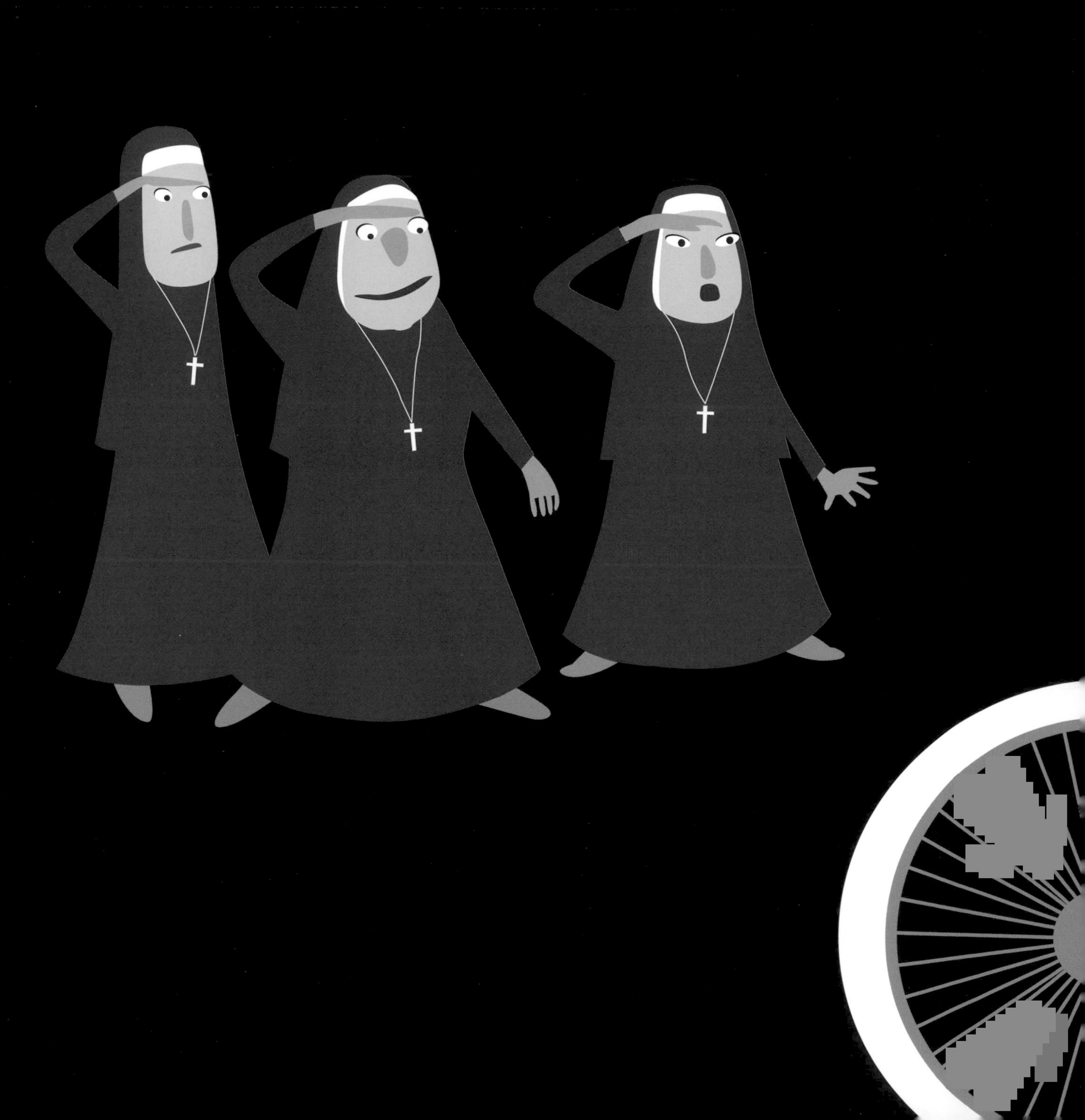

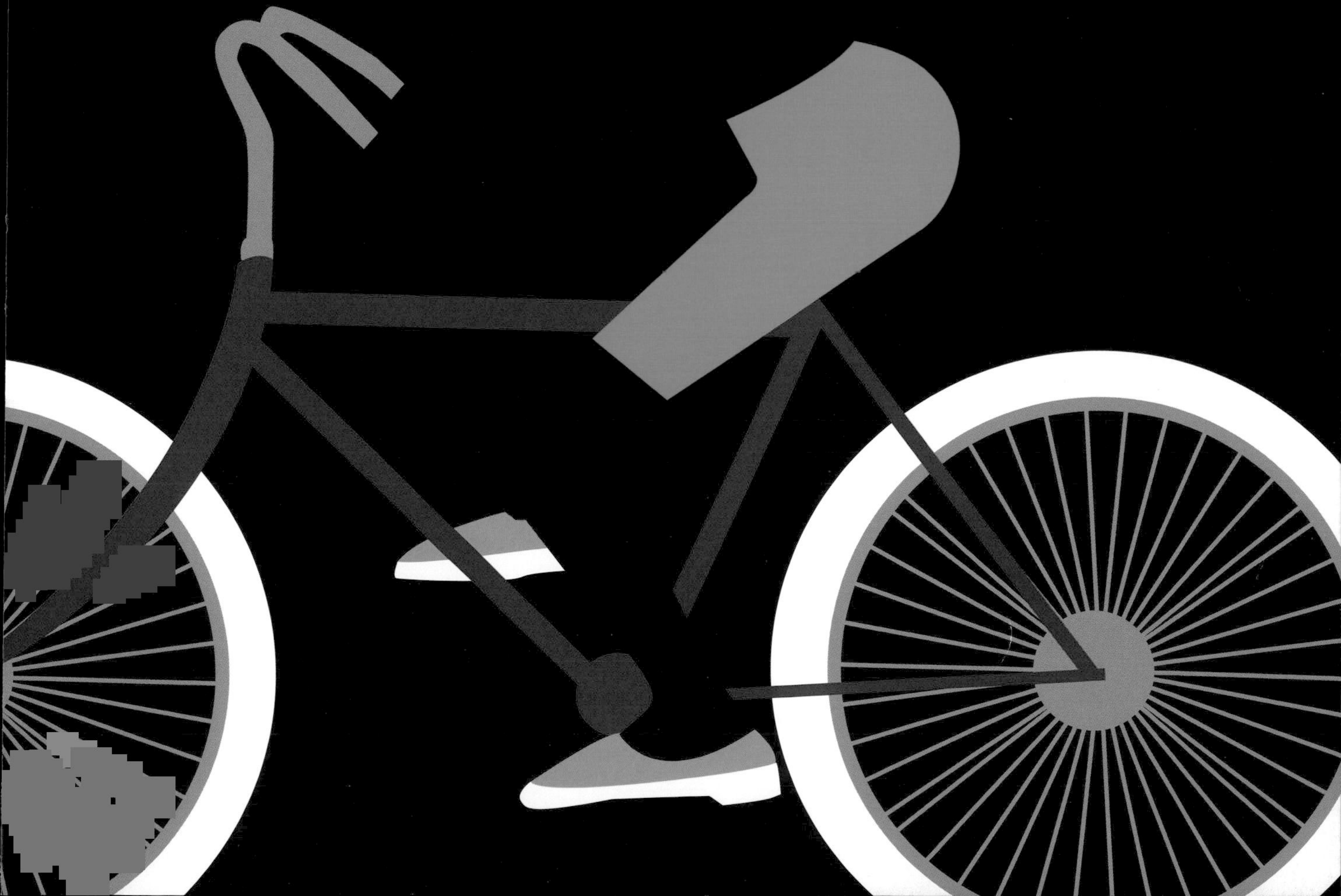

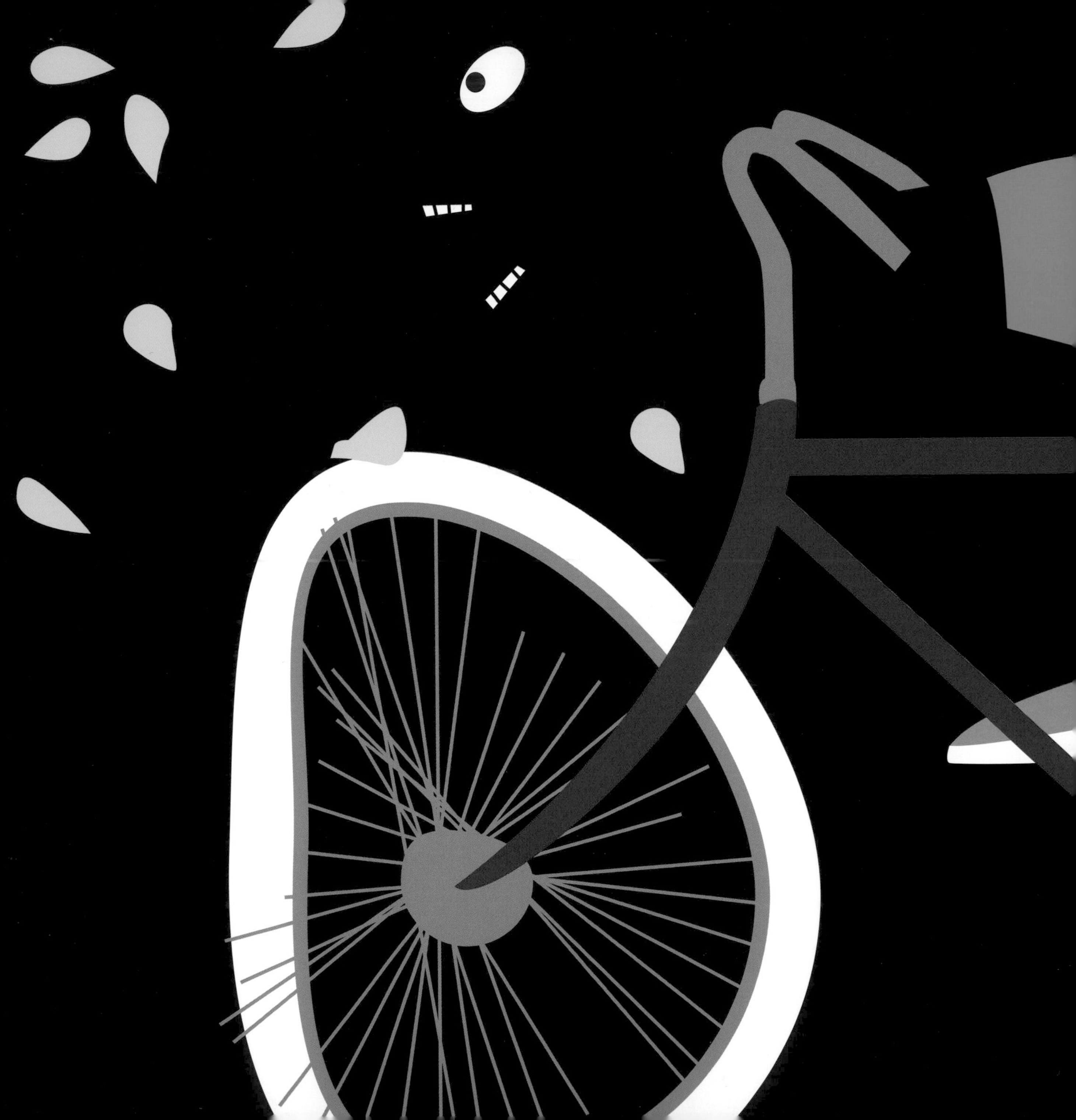

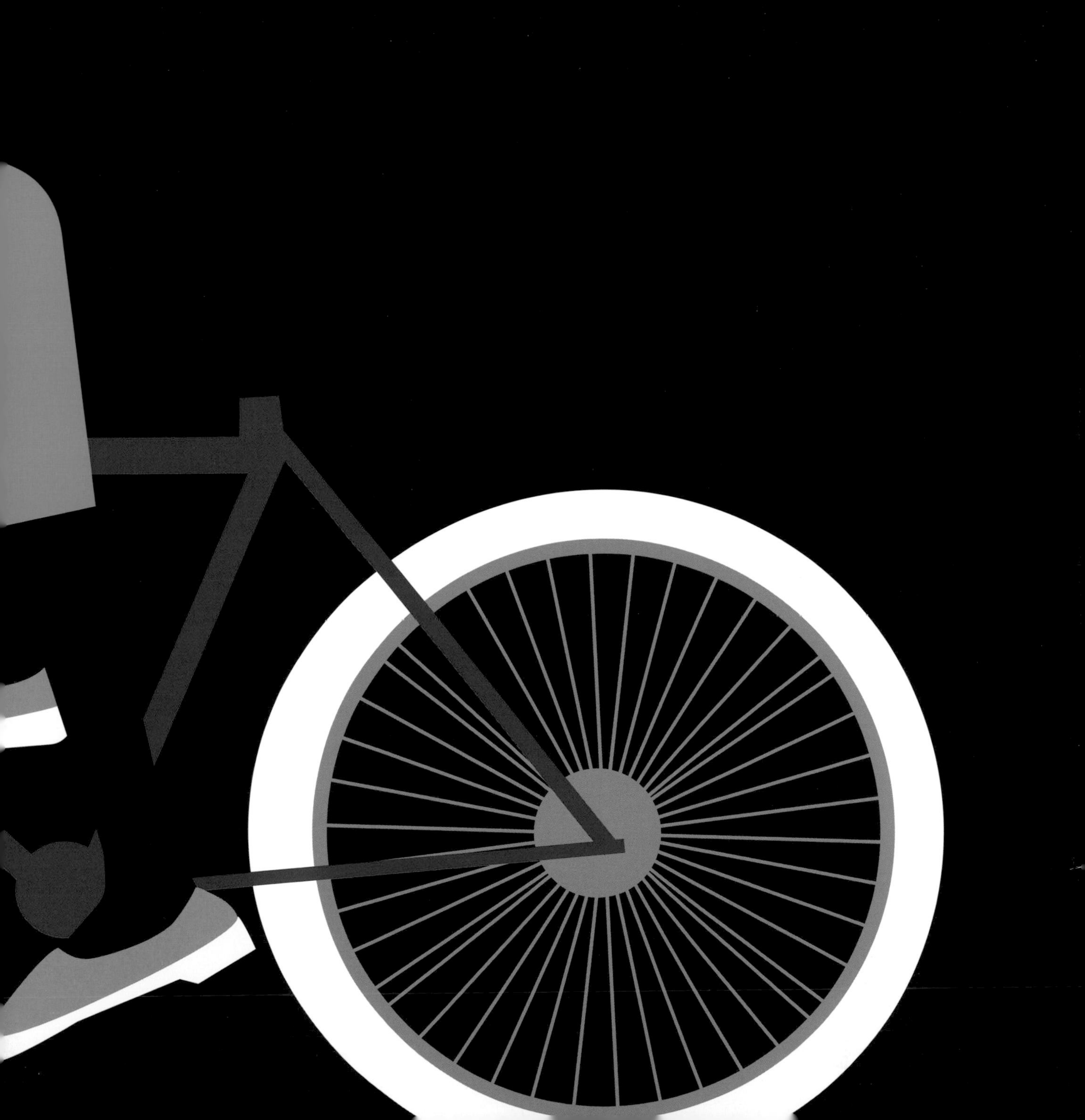

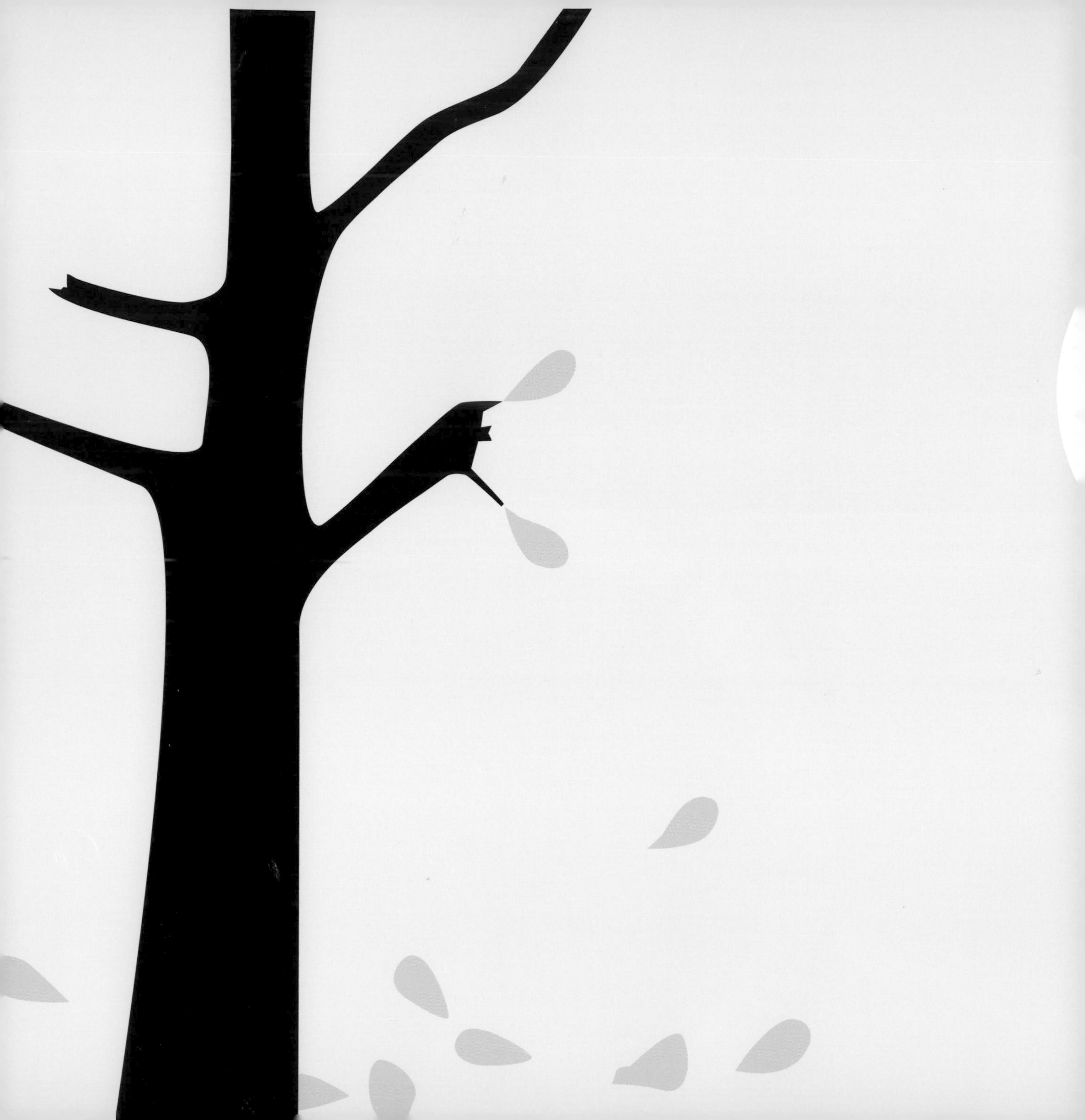

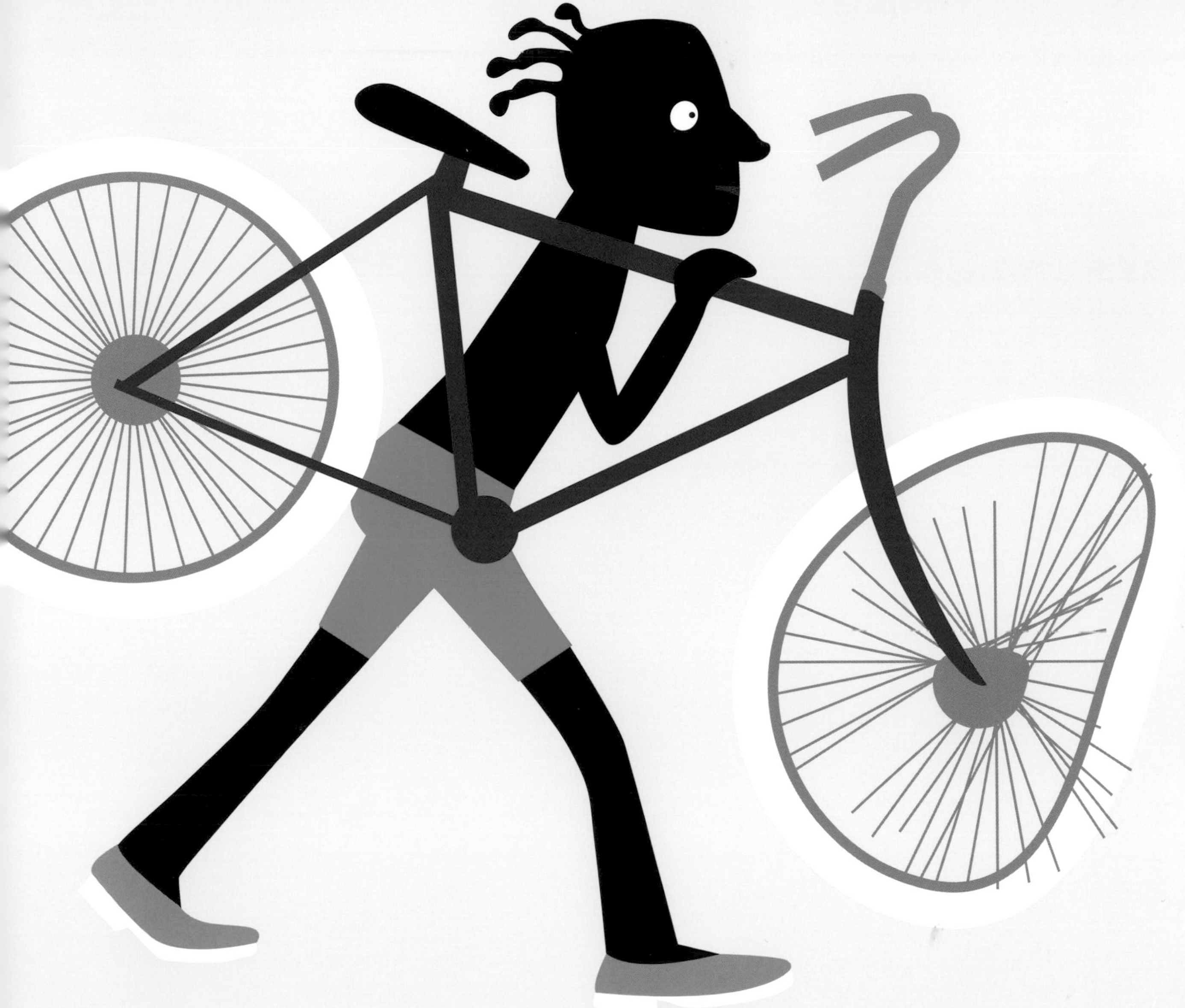

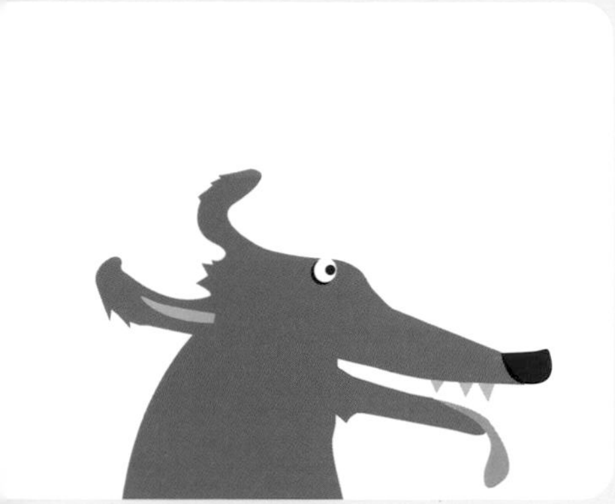
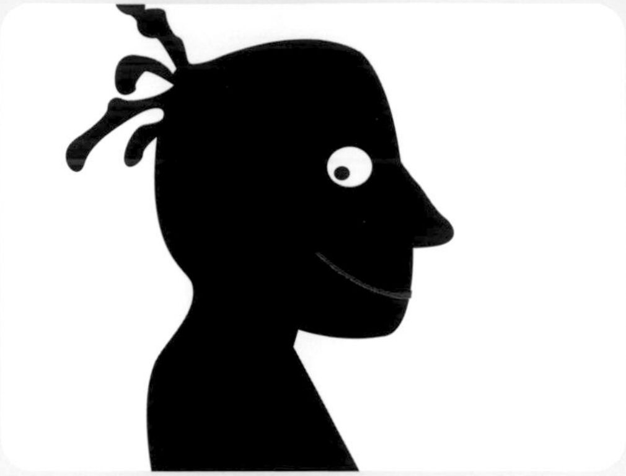
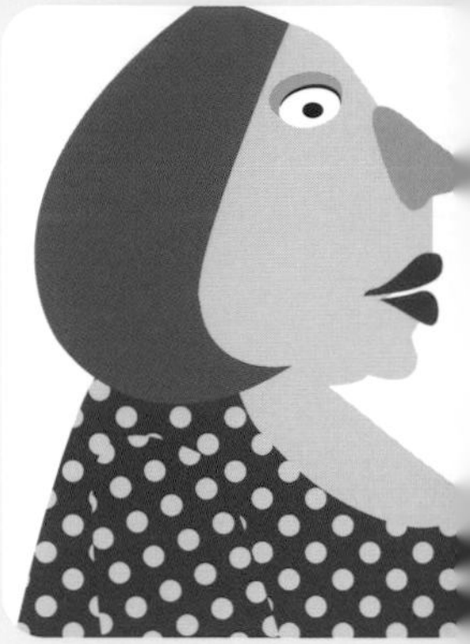

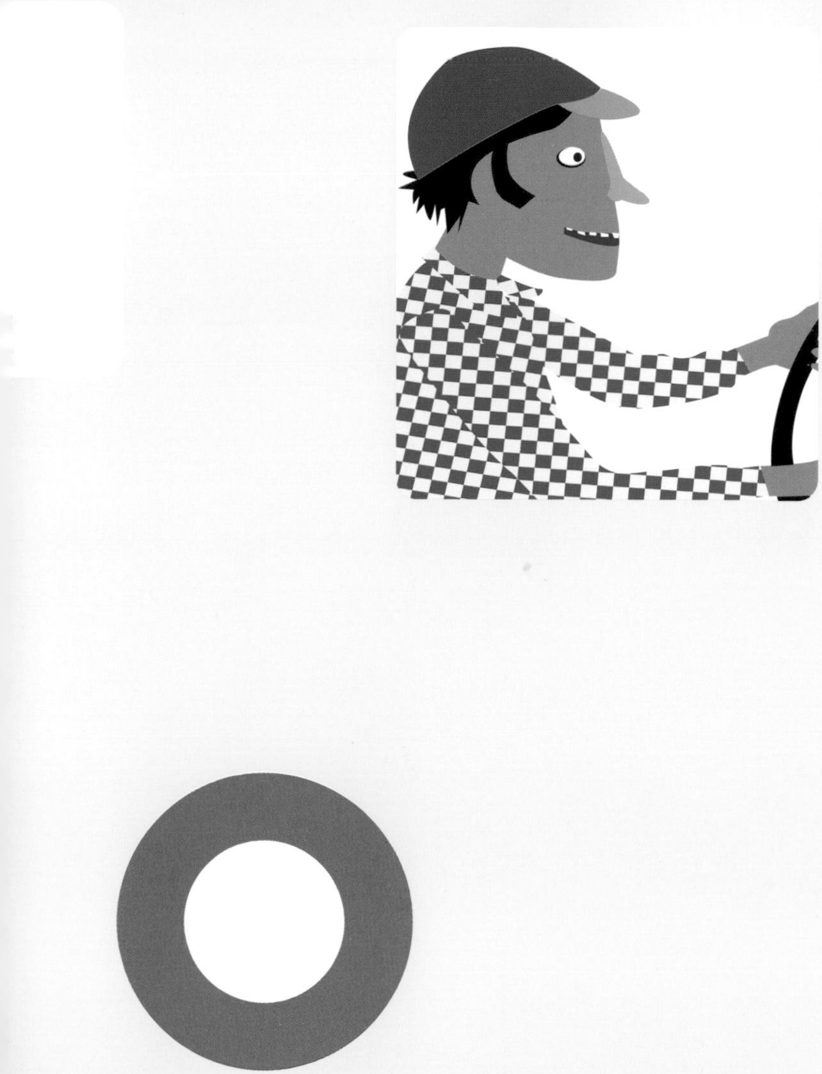

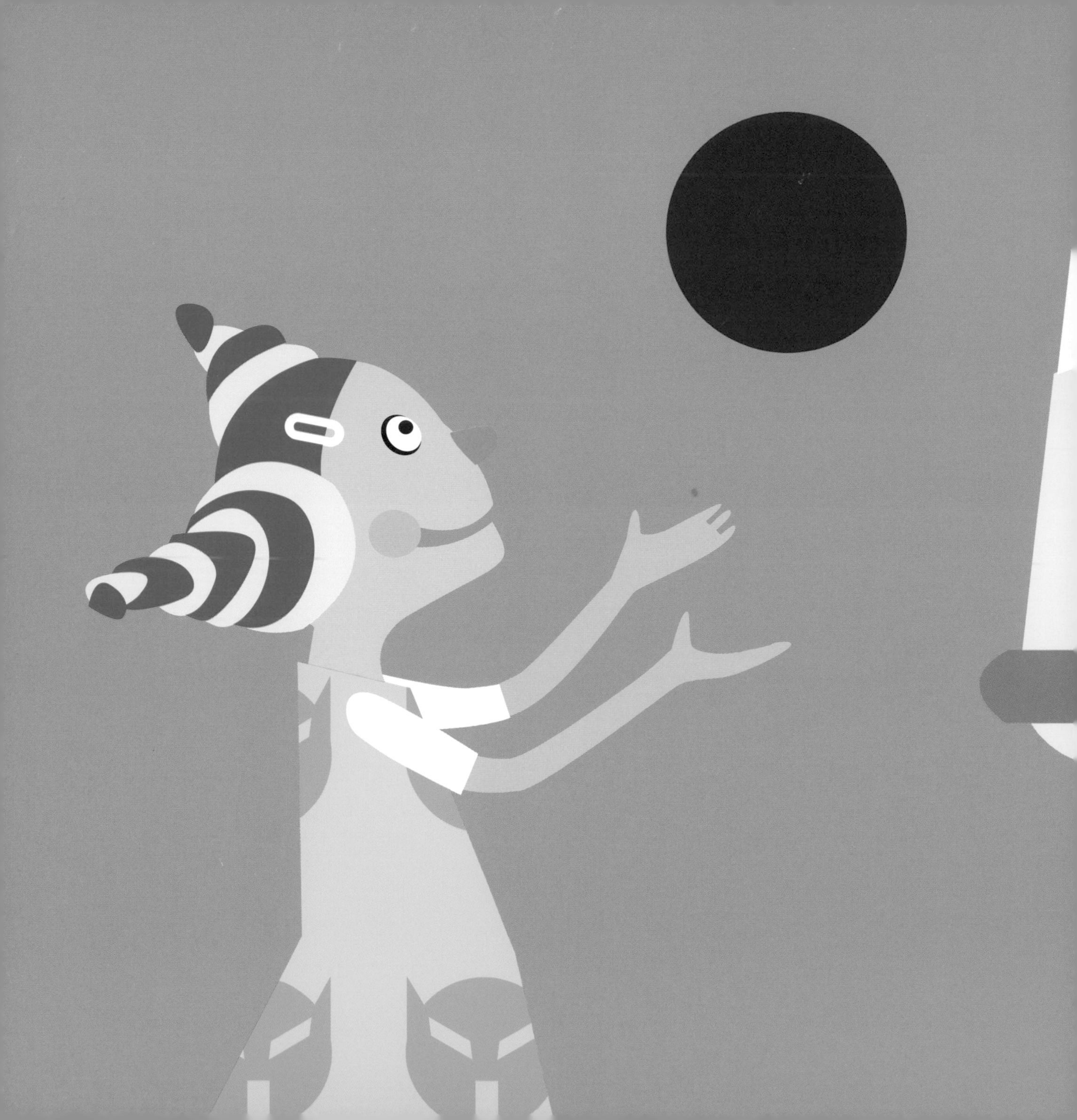

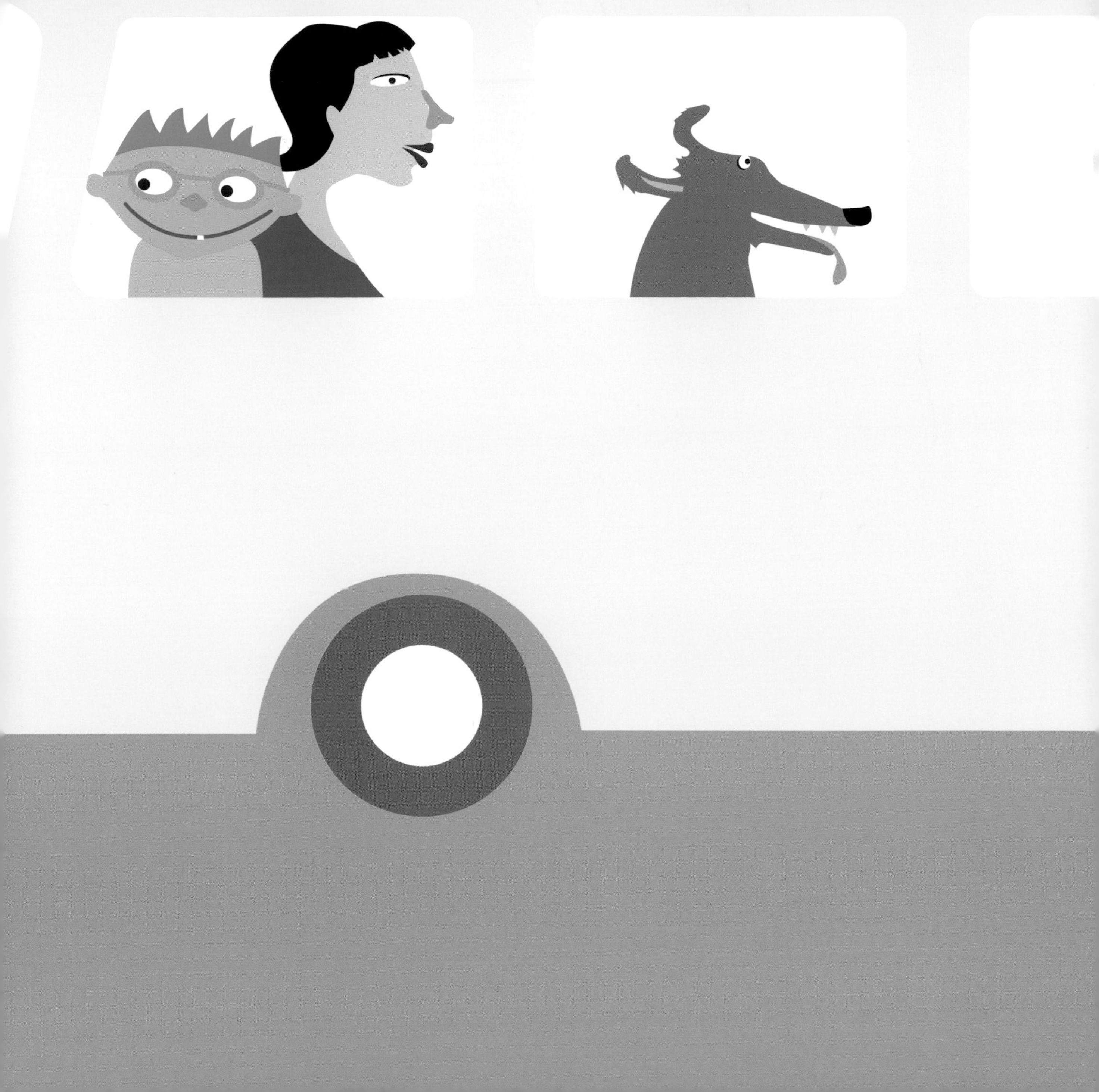

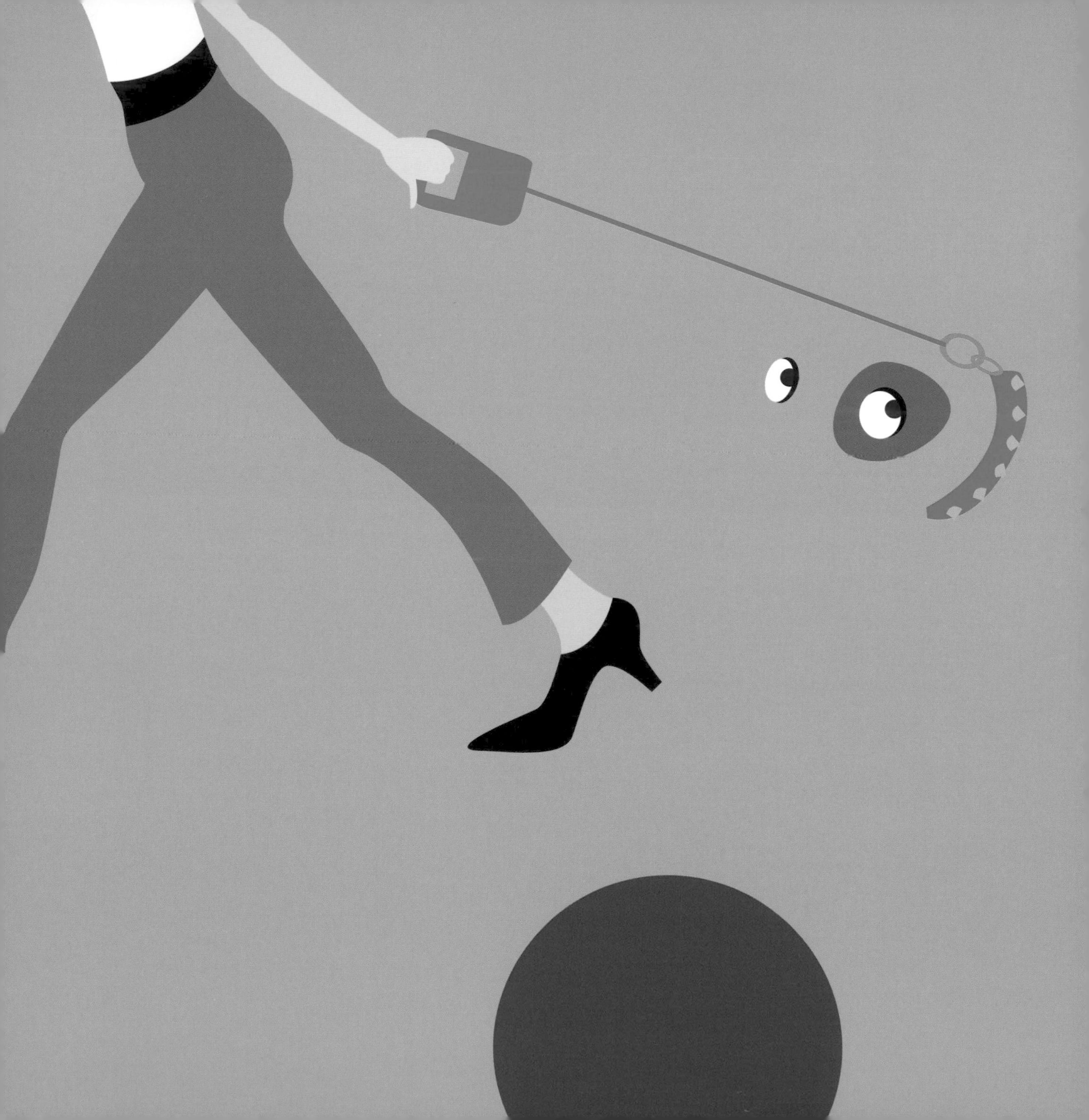

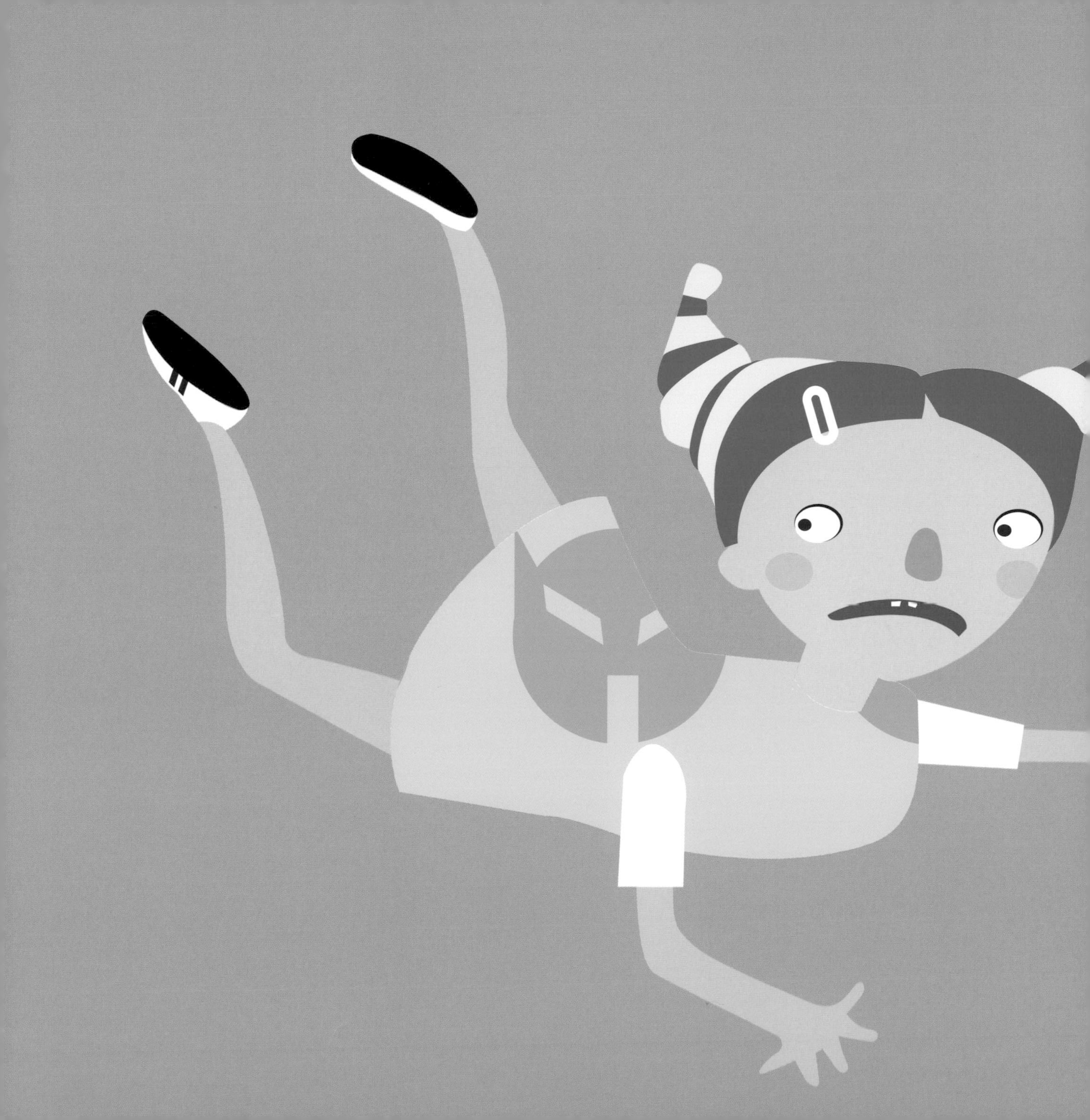

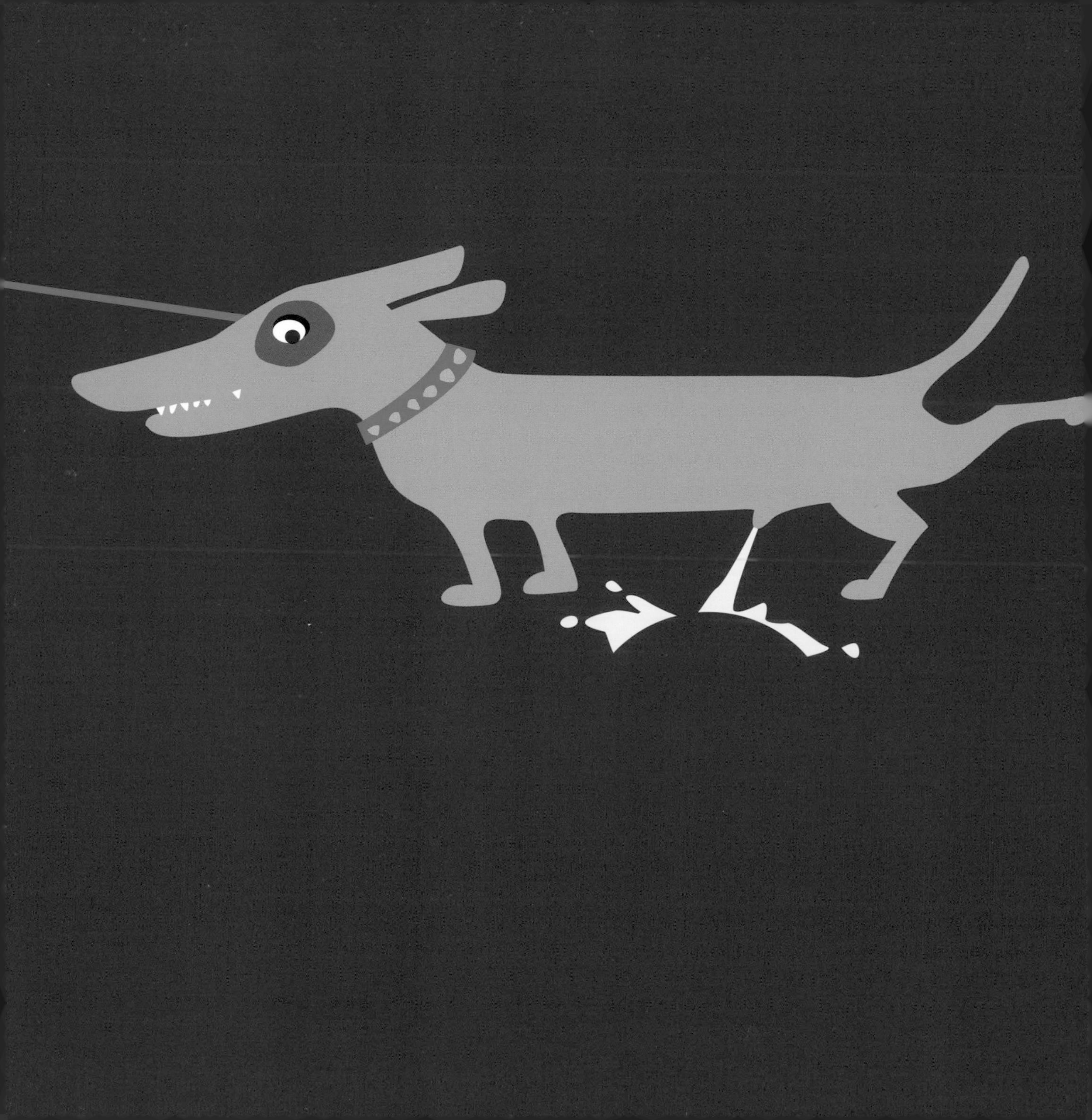

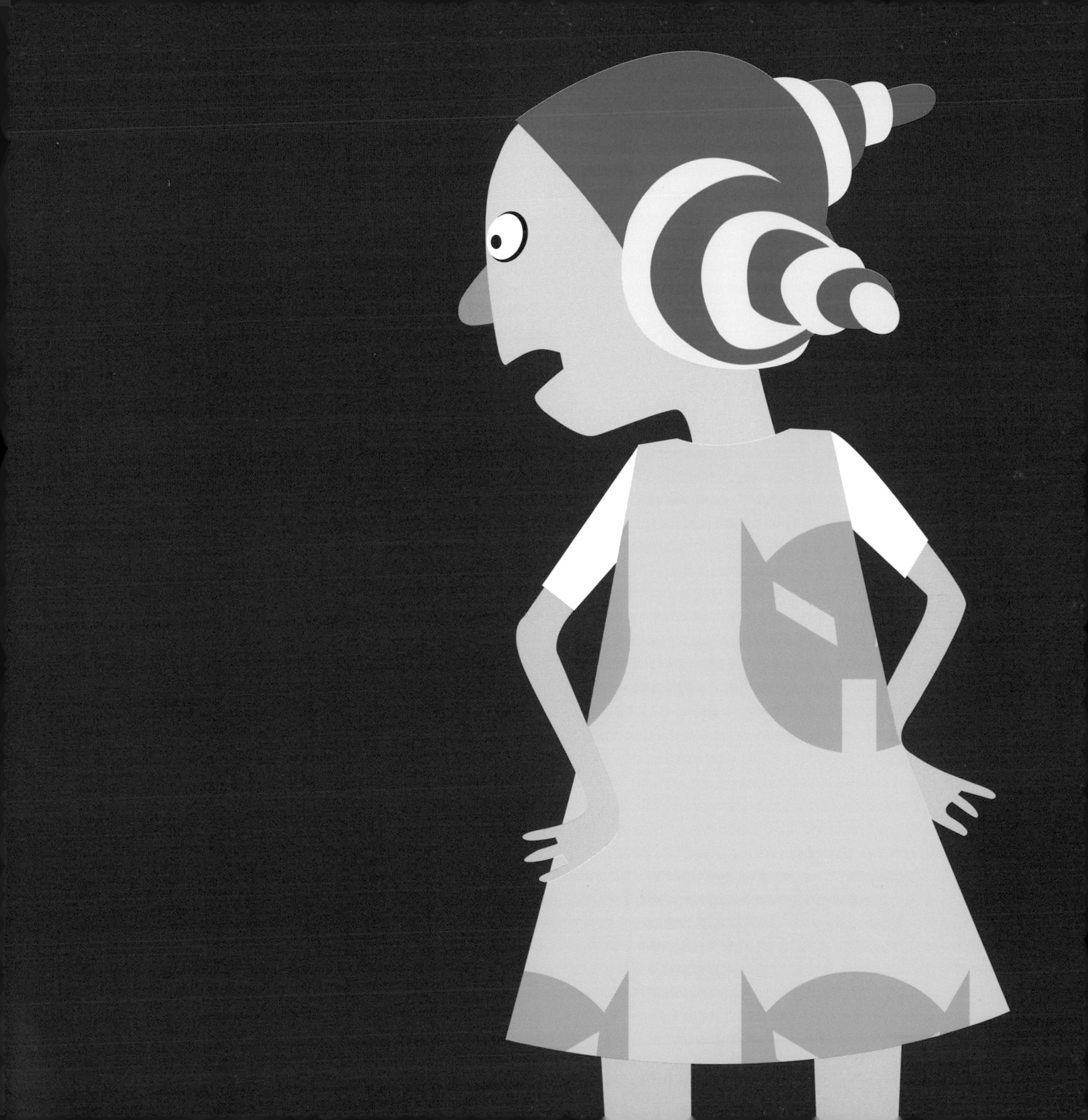

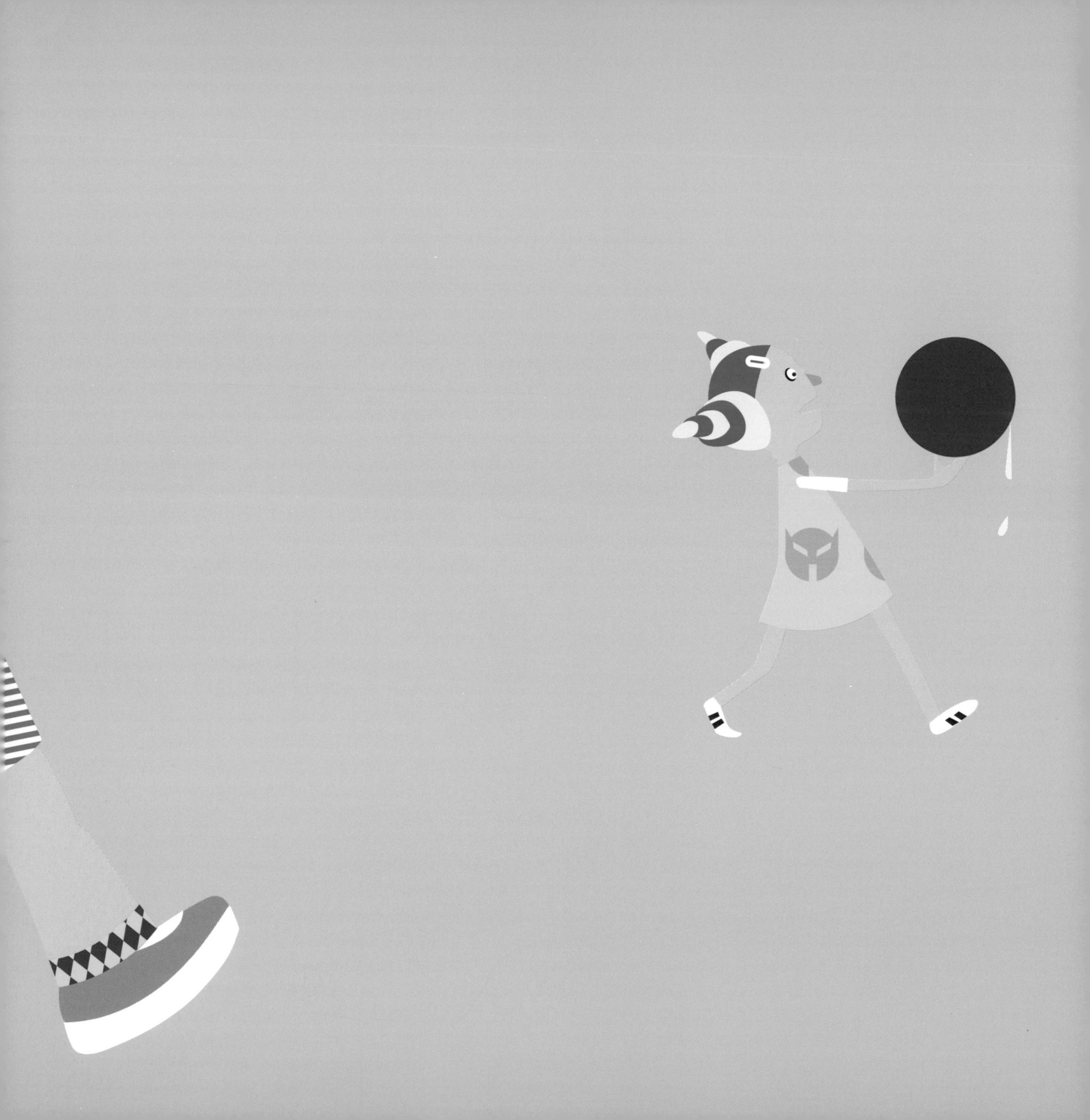

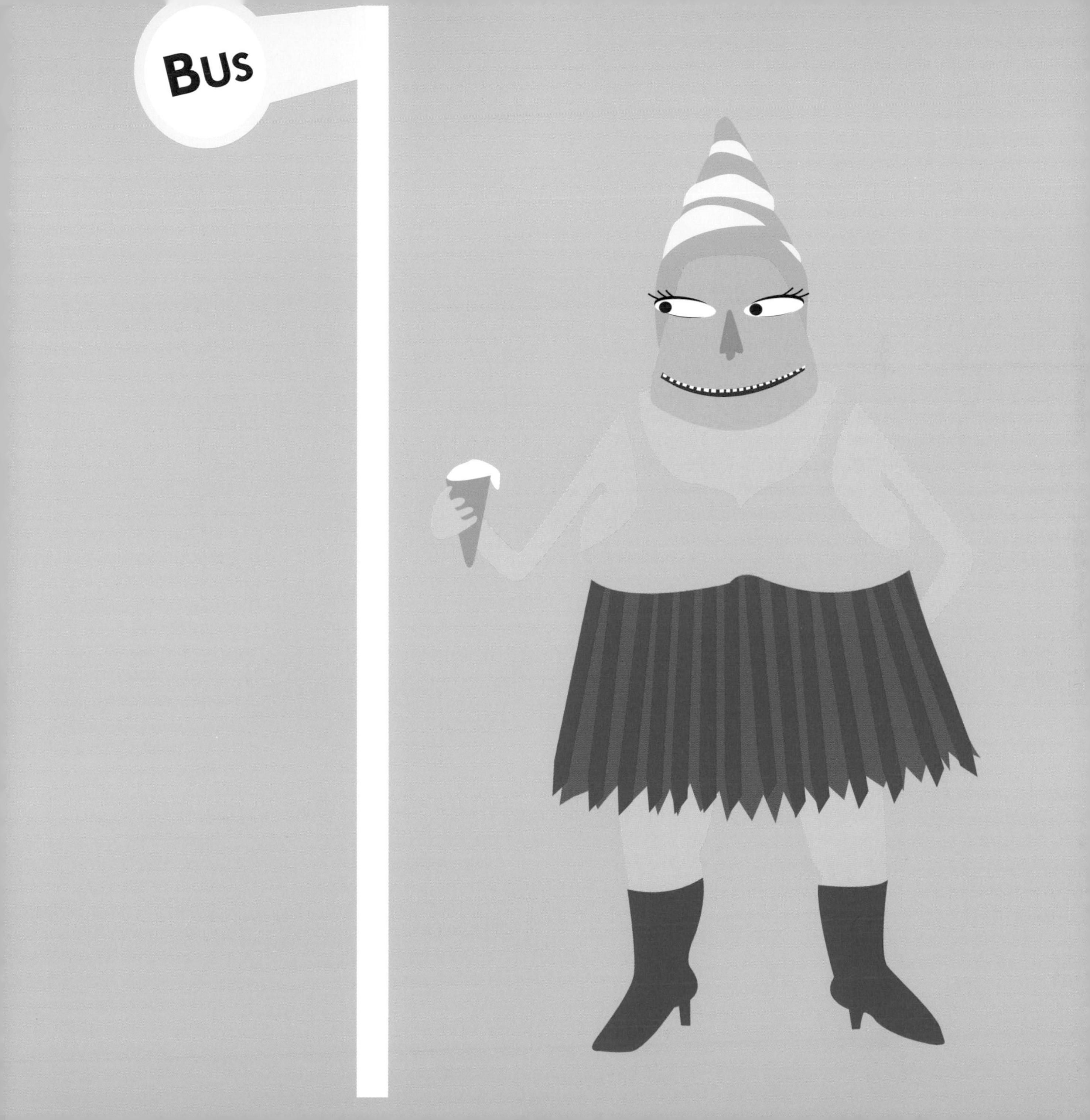
BUS

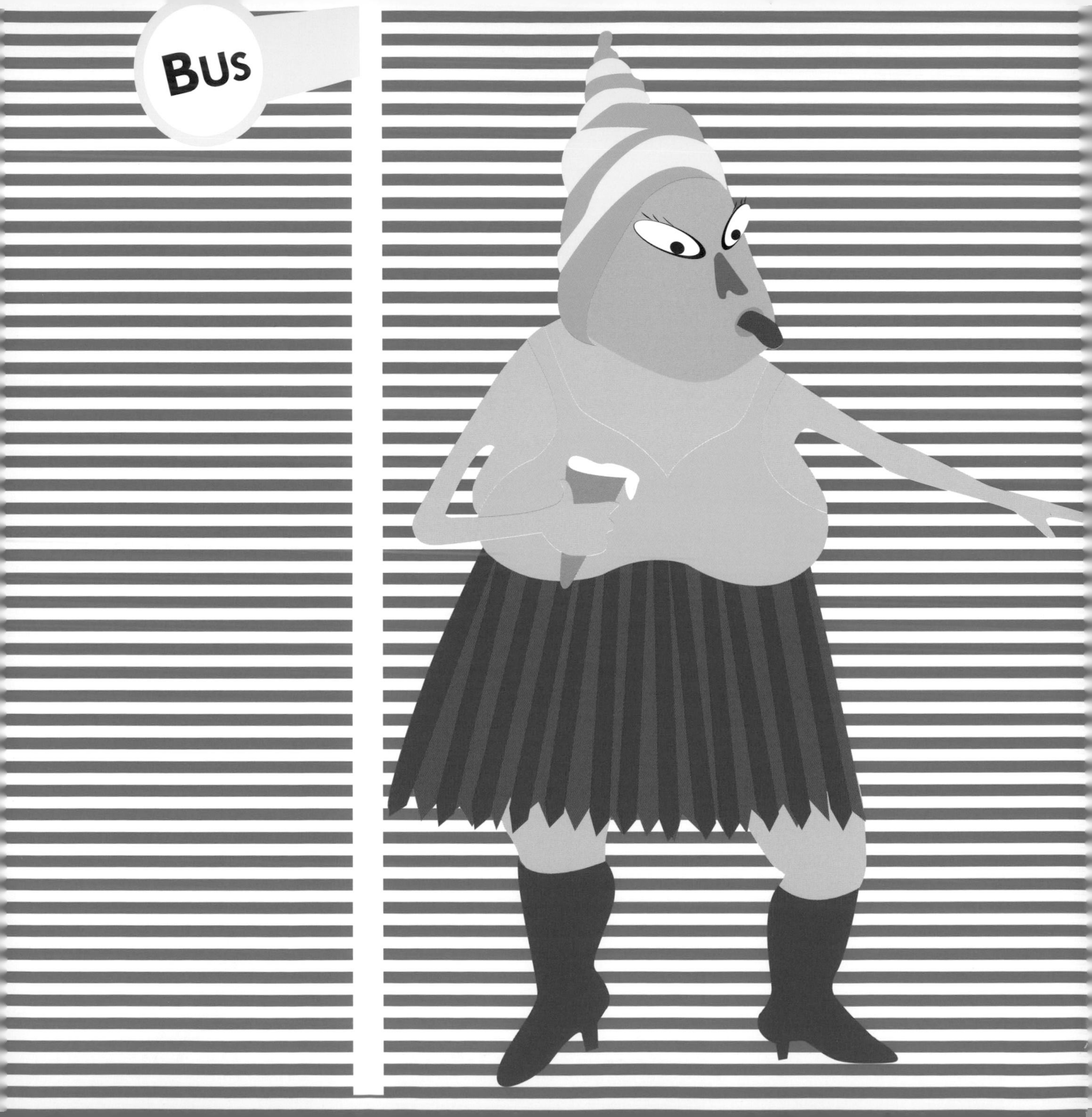
BUS

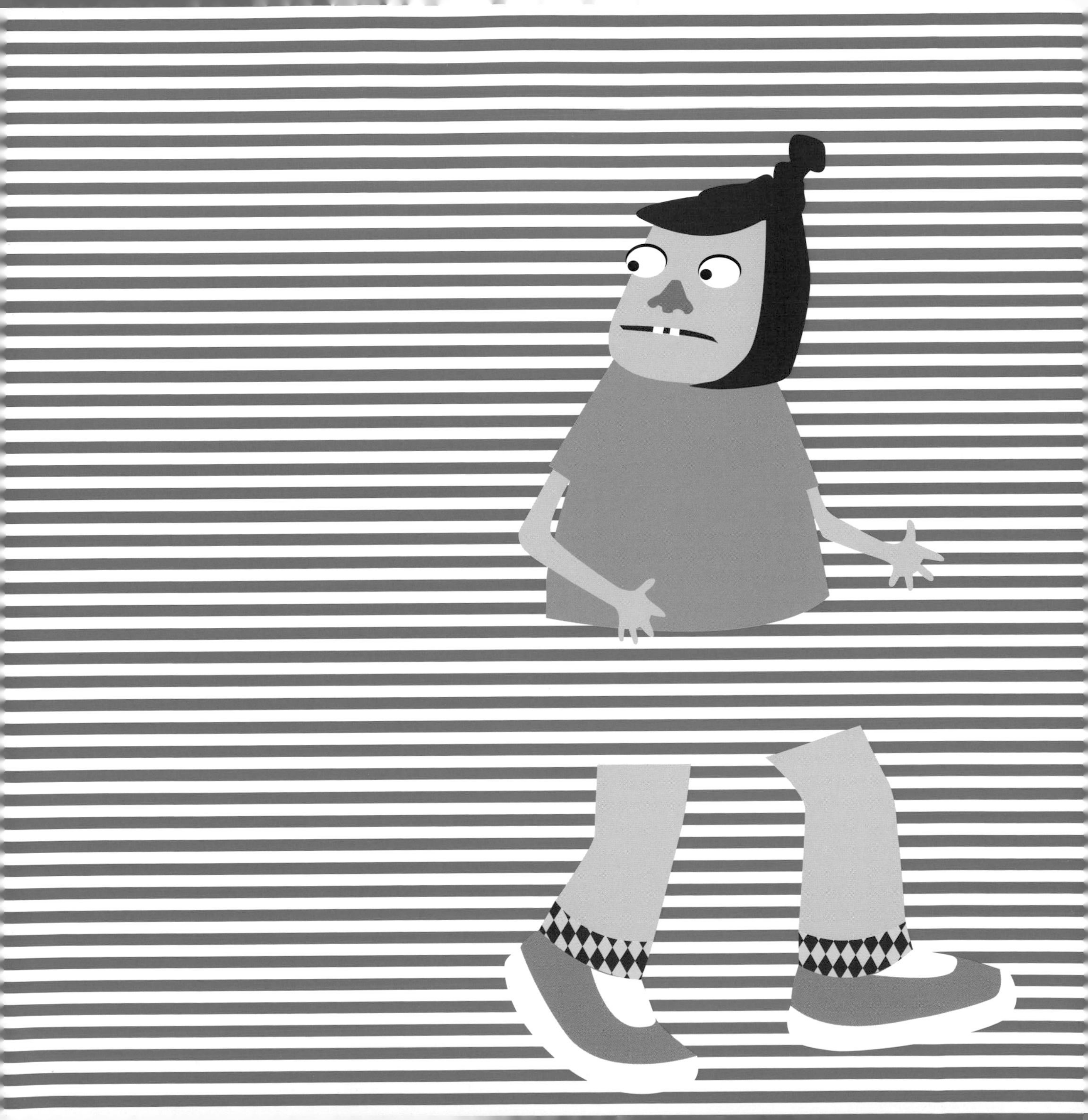

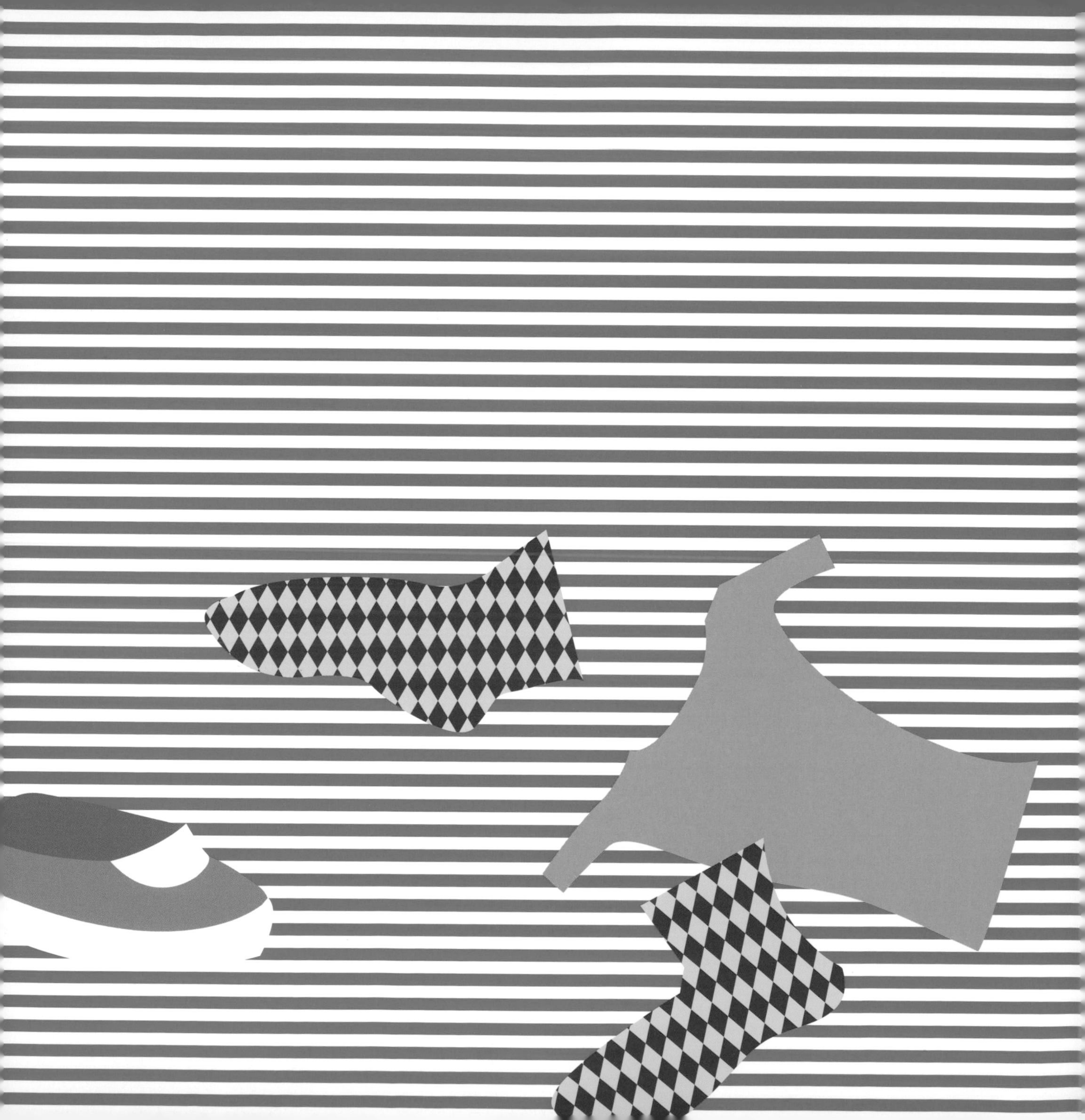

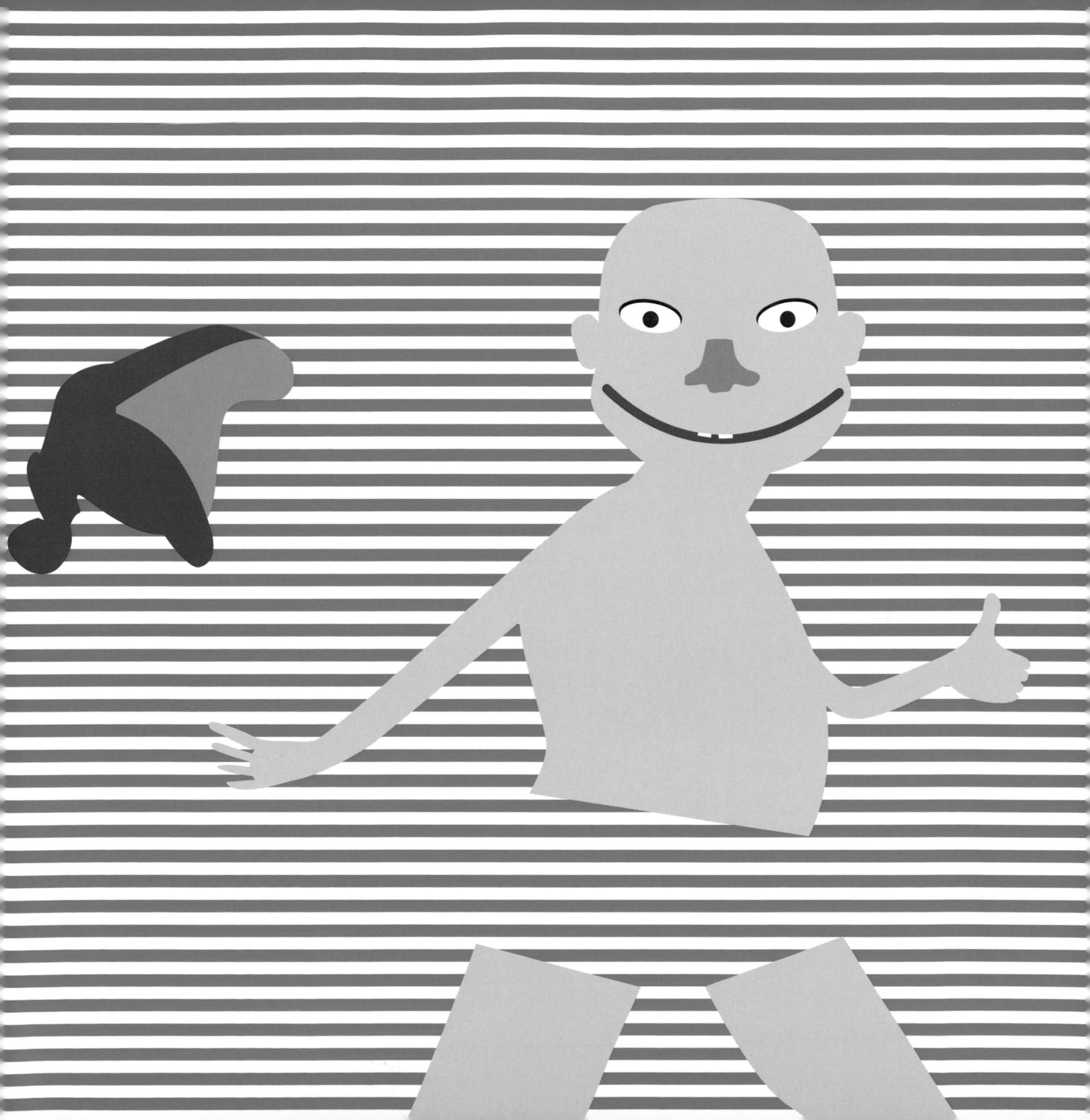

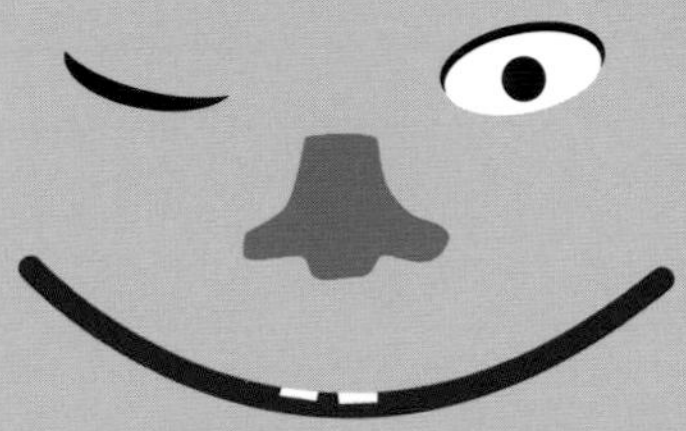